KU-799-815

Paddington
the Artist

First published in hardback in Great Britain by HarperCollins Publishers Ltd in 1985
First published in paperback by Collins Picture Books in 2000
Revised paperback edition published by HarperCollins Children's Books in 2009
This edition published as part of a set in 2014

Collins Picture Books is an imprint of HarperCollins Publishers Ltd.
HarperCollins Children's Books is a division of HarperCollins Publishers Ltd.

Text copyright © Michael Bond 1985
Illustrations copyright © R. W. Alley 1998

The author and illustrator assert the moral right to be identified as the author and illustrator of the work.
A CIP catalogue record for this title is available from the British Library. All rights reserved. No part of this
publication may be reproduced, stored in a retrieval system or transmitted in any form or by any means,
electronic, mechanical, photocopying, recording or otherwise, without the prior permission of
HarperCollins Publishers Ltd, 1 London Bridge Street, London SE1 9GF.

Visit our website at: www.harpercollins.co.uk

Printed in China

Michael Bond
Paddington
the Artist

Illustrated by R. W. Alley

HarperCollins *Children's Books*

One Sunday Paddington was out for a walk with his friend Mr Gruber, when they came across some paintings tied to the railings outside the park.

"It's what is known as an Outdoor
Exhibition," said Mr Gruber. "They have
one here every week when the weather
is nice."

"All the paintings are for sale," Mr Gruber explained. "This one is called 'Sunset in Bombay'."

"I'm glad I don't live in Bombay," said Paddington. "It might keep me awake all night."

"How about this one then?" said Mr Gruber.
"It's called 'Storm at Sea'."

Paddington suddenly wished he hadn't
eaten such a big breakfast.

"I feel sick," he said, and he hurried
on to the next picture.

"This is a picture the artist painted of himself," said Mr Gruber. "It's called a self-portrait. I think it looks very like him."

Paddington gave the picture a hard stare.

"I don't think I'll buy any paintings today, Mr Gruber," he said.

Paddington looked very thoughtful as he made his way back home to number thirty-two Windsor Gardens.

When he got there, Paddington collected all
his paints and brushes from his room and
went out into the garden.

The next Sunday, when he and Mr Gruber had finished their walk, Paddington led the way back towards Windsor Gardens.

"I'm having an Outdoor Exhibition of my own this week, Mr Gruber," he said.

"This is meant to be a sunset in Windsor Gardens. Only it took me quite a long time and it got dark before I could finish it.

"And this is a picture of a rainstorm, only it got very wet and all the paint ran."

"This is my best one," said Paddington. "It's a picture of me. I've put my special paw mark on to show I painted it myself."

Mr Gruber gazed at Paddington's portrait for a long time.

"It is very good, Mr Brown," he said at last, not wishing to upset his friend, "but I think you look even better in real life."

"I kept going upstairs to look at myself in the mirror," said Paddington, "but by the time I got downstairs again I'd forgotten what I looked like."

"Painting isn't as easy as it looks," Paddington
added sadly, "especially with paws. I think
I might give up."

"I hope you don't do that, Mr Brown,"
Mr Gruber said thoughtfully.

After Mr Gruber had said goodbye, Paddington sat down beside his paintings hoping that someone would stop and buy one.

But it was a warm day and no one came past.
In the end Paddington fell asleep.

When he woke up, Paddington found to his surprise that all his pictures had gone.

But tucked inside his duffle coat he found an envelope with his name on: Mr Paddington Brown, 32 Windsor Gardens. And inside the envelope there was some money and a note saying 'Thank you'.

If Mr and Mrs Brown recognised Mr Gruber's
writing they didn't say anything. They hadn't
had such a peaceful time for ages.

And best of all, Paddington carried on painting.
So everyone was happy.

"I think I may paint a family portrait now," said Paddington. "That is, if I have enough paint left for all the smiles."

Look out for more fantastic
picture books about Paddington!

Paddington

Paddington in the Garden

Paddington and the Grand Tour

Paddington at the Carnival

Paddington and the Christmas Surprise

Paddington Goes for Gold

Paddington and the Marmalade Maze

Paddington at the Zoo

Paddington at the Tower

Paddington at the Palace

Paddington and the Disappearing Sandwich

Paddington – King of the Castle

Paddington at the Rainbow's End

HarperCollins *Children's Books*

www.harpercollins.co.uk